retold by John Warren Stewig

illustratd by Margot Tomes

Holiday House / New York

·STONE SOUP·

Library of Congress Cataloging-in-Publication Data
Stewig, John W.
Stone soup / adapted by John Warren Stewig ; illustrated by
Margot Tomes.—1st ed.
p.   cm.
Summary: A clever lass, in need of a meal, shows some stingy
villagers how to make soup starting with a magic stone.
[1. Folklore—France.]   I. Tomes, Margot, ill.   II. Title.
PZ8.1.S8574St   1991
398.21′0944—dc20
[E]   90-46502   CIP   AC
ISBN 0-8234-0863-9

To Mrs. Roberts, children's librarian,
who in that Carnegie Library children's room
started me on a journey

J.W.S.

For Margery Cuyler, gratefully

M.T.

No one loved Grethel more than her mother. And no one loved her mother more than Grethel. They were happy together scratching out a poor living from their small farm. But despite their hard work, the day came when the farm would no longer support the two of them. So one day Grethel decided that she should set off down the road. Perhaps, being clever, she could discover a way to make life easier for her mother and herself.

Day broke bright the next morning. Grethel's mother packed her a picnic of bread and cheese. "Now be careful, and don't stay away too long," she said. Then she hugged Grethel before she started down the road to see what she could see.

The first day went well, as did the second. But by the third day, Grethel had eaten all her food. Her stomach was as hollow as a scooped-out pumpkin. She was hungry! Ahead on the road she could see a village. Perhaps there she could find supper and a warm place to sleep.

Grethel stopped at the first house near the edge of the village. "Good evening," she said politely. "Could you spare some food for a hungry traveler?"

"Oh, we've little enough for ourselves," said the peasant. "The harvest was poor this year."

No sooner had the man closed the door than he bid his wife go through the backyard to warn the neighbors.

Word spread quickly from house to house that a young traveler was in the village asking for food.

Now, the people in the village were stingy. As soon as they heard the news, they hid whatever they had. They covered the sacks of barley and corn in their barns with hay. They lowered their milk down their wells.

They hid their cabbages and potatoes in small cupboards under their stairs. They hung their meat from the rafters in their cellars. After they'd hidden all they had to eat, they put on long faces, in order to look hungry.

By this time, Grethel had stopped at a house near the center of the village and knocked at the door. She politely asked the peasant who answered if he could spare a heel of bread and a rind of cheese.

"Oh, no," replied the villager, turning down the corners of his mouth like an unlucky horseshoe. "Just last week three weary soldiers passed through our village, and we gave them what little we could spare."

Grethel thanked the villager and made her way to a
house on the edge of the town square. But again she was
told there was no food to spare.

"I have an old, sick uncle to care for," said the villager, "so I already have an extra mouth to feed."

Throughout the village, all the peasants had good excuses. One family had to feed their extra grain to their livestock. Another had to sell their extra food at the market to buy winter clothes for their children. Yet a third was helping a brother's family that had fallen on hard times. All had too many mouths to feed.

Discouraged, Grethel sat down on a bench in the town square. "I am growing hungrier by the minute," she thought. "I have to come up with something." As she thought, Grethel looked down at the gravel under her feet. She noticed a large, smooth stone. Suddenly, she had an idea.

She stood and called to a few villagers walking past the square.

"Good folk," she said as the peasants drew near. "I am but a poor, hungry lass, out to seek my fortune. Until I find it, I must ask for help. Since you have no food, we'll just have to use my magic stone to make stone soup."

The peasants leaned forward. Stone soup? Surely that was impossible.

"First we'll need a large iron pot," Grethel said.

The peasants searched throughout the village and brought the largest one they could find.

"That's none too large," said Grethel, "but it will do. And now we'll need water to fill it and fire to heat it."

The villagers brought many buckets of water to fill the pot. They built a fire on the village square and set the pot to boil. When the water was boiling, the villagers watched as Grethel dropped the stone into the water. Grethel stirred the soup, tasted it, and stirred some more.

"This soup needs a bit of salt and pepper," said Grethel.

A mother nudged her two children, and they ran off to fetch some. When they returned, they helped Grethel shake it into the pot.

"This magic stone always makes excellent soup. But I sometimes help it along by adding a carrot or two, to make it tastier," said Grethel.

"Why, I think I can give you a few carrots," said one of the peasant women, hurrying away. She brought back all the carrots that lay hidden beneath the quilt on her bed.

"A good stone soup needs a bit of cabbage," said Gre-thel, as she sliced the carrots into the pot. "But no use asking for what you don't have."

"I think I know where I can find a cabbage," said another peasant woman, running home. Back she came with three cabbages that she fetched from the cupboard beneath her stairs. She helped slice the cabbages into the soup.

Grethel stirred and tasted, wrinkling her nose in pleasure over the tasty smell.

"If only we had a shank of beef and a few small potatoes, this soup would be good enough for a nobleman's table."

The peasants thought about that. They remembered sacks of potatoes in dark corners and sides of beef hanging in musty cellars. They ran to get them.

A nobleman's soup—and all from a magic stone. It seemed impossible!

"Ah," said Grethel, stirring in the beef and potatoes, "if only we could add a little barley and a cup of milk. Then this soup would be good enough for the king himself. Indeed when last we dined, he complimented me on just such a soup."

The peasants whispered to each other, "Grethel has eaten with the king! Well! How extraordinary!"

"But no use asking for what you don't have," Grethel said with a sigh.

The peasants brought barley from their lofts and milk from where it was hidden in their wells. Grethel slowly added the barley and milk to the steaming broth. The peasants watched until, at last, the soup was ready.

"Everyone shall eat," said Grethel. "But first we must set a table."

The peasants carried great tables into the square and lit torches all around them. The soup smelled so delicious!

As they waited, the peasants talked among themselves. "Does not such a fine soup require bread—and a roast—and cider? Then it will surely be fit for a king." They went off to prepare a banquet, and finally everyone sat down to eat.

Never had the villagers shared such a feast. Never had they tasted such soup. And imagine, made from a stone!

They ate and drank, and after that they sang and danced. At last they were so tired that they began to head for their cottages. Then Grethel asked, "Is there a barn with an empty haymow, where I can sleep until morning?"

"Let such a wise and clever cook sleep in a haymow? No indeed," cried the town folk. Nothing would do but that Grethel went off with the mayor and his wife to sleep in a feather bed higher and softer than she had ever dreamed possible.

In the morning, the entire village gathered in the square to wish Grethel well as she continued on her journey.

"Many thanks for sharing your magic soup stone with us," a peasant said to Grethel. "That was an evening, and a soup to remember."

"Oh, it was nothing," replied Grethel. "In fact, since you enjoyed the soup, I'll leave you my stone, so you can make soup together whenever you wish."

The villagers were delighted with such generosity, and sent Grethel packing, her sack bulging with food and good wishes. They waved her down the path, sorry to see such an up-and-coming young lass go on her way.

As the path curved down the hill, out of sight of the village, Grethel picked up a small, smooth stone to take back to her mother. "Now I know how to keep food on our table," she mused. And much refreshed, she marched down the road toward home.